Born and raised near Doncaster, **Liz Sabin** hasn't had it easy but has never been one to give up.
She spent most of her childhood holidays in South Wales, visiting her Granny.
If her head is not in a book, she can usually be found baking cakes or walking the dog.

Copyright © 2021 Liz Sabin

All rights reserved.

ISBN: 9798452459743

Coastal Expressions

Liz Sabin

With my Heartfelt Thanks
to all my Family, Friends and Medical Professionals
who have and continue,
to help and support me
through the good times and the bad times

CHAPTER ONE

Tucked in one of the books Megan had brought with her to read, was a small photo. Carefully she slid it out. As she held the photo, a tear fell onto it, which she gently wiped away. After all this time it still broke her heart to remember those wonderful times spent learning the most beautiful skill.

"Breakfast is ready" came from downstairs and interrupted her thoughts.

She got up, carefully slid the photo back into the book and wiped her eyes, before heading downstairs.

"I'm on my way granny" she shouted back, as she carefully descended the stairs and joined her for breakfast.

After they had finished breakfast, granny asked her to see if the post had come as she was waiting for her daily newspaper, which the postman kindly delivered with the post, to read.

She headed out of the front door and turned to the box next to it. Carefully she climbed up onto the stone wall beneath it. One of these days I won't need to climb up to see into the box, she thought to herself, while wishing she wasn't so small, as she reached for the lid. The lid creaked as she lifted it up.

"I haven't put the post in yet!!"

She jumped and turned, almost losing her balance, to see a young man reaching out to steady her before she fell.

"I'm really sorry, I didn't mean to startle you" he said with a smooth welsh accent.

As they both got steady on their feet, she smiled nervously "Its ok and thank you"

"You are very welcome, oh and a drop of oil should sort your hinges out!!"

She look at him shocked "My hinges?!"

"I'm so sorry I meant the hinges on the post box!!" he worriedly replied and then he saw the amused smile on her face. "You are winding me up aren't you?"

She nodded and they both laughed.

"Ah you've met my granddaughter then?"

They both jumped.

"Hello there, yes, well sort of. Hi, I'm Caerwyn"

She suddenly realized she was stood there, staring at him, he was ruggedly handsome in a red mail t-shirt. She went to reply, only to meet his gaze and couldn't get her words out.

"This is my granddaughter Megan, She is a little bit shy" granny chipped in with a smile.

Neither of them replied instead they just stood there, gazing at each other.

"Megan has come to look after me" granny continued.

Realizing he was being spoken too, he pulled himself together. "That's good, it's always handy to have an extra pair of hands" he smiled back.

"Well I don't know about that, this one is like a bull in a china shop at the best of times!!" granny laughed.

"Granny stop embarrassing me" Megan suddenly found her voice again. "I think you better go and sit down" she said ushering her away from the door.

"That's me told!!" granny winked and started moving away from the door.

"That's ok, I better get on, see you both later" he said and turned to walk back towards the post van, stopping at the end of the drive, he turned "Oh and nice to meet you Megan, I hope you get your hinges oiled!!" he winked and with a little chuckle, turned back around and carried on to the post van.

"Bye and nice to meet you too Caerwyn" she replied with a nervous smile and headed back inside with the post.

"Nice young man that Caerwyn, don't you think?" granny said as Megan sat down at the kitchen table.

"Yes I suppose so" she muttered as she passed granny her newspaper.

Megan then opened the local newspaper that was in front of her. As she flicked through it, a small advert caught her eye. The picture on it was a couple of dancers in a dance pose, which brought the memories back again and she fought back the tears in her eyes.

She looked at the rest of the advert, it was offering a dance class, in a hall in Cardiff Bay, on Thursday evenings from 7pm to 8pm. She thought for a moment, maybe she could go and see what it's like but then she remembered why she couldn't and decided against it. Closing the newspaper, she got up and went to get ready to clean the house.

A few days past and several times Megan had bumped into Caerwyn on the doorstep, where they managed timidly to talk about different things, like the weather and what was happening in the neighborhood.

The dance advert was still playing on Megan's mind. Several times she had thought about going but she just couldn't bring herself to go.

CHAPTER TWO

Thursday evening came around and Megan had been working late, helping her cousin, preparing food for a wedding, that her cousin's company was providing the catering for, which she enjoyed doing and it gave her a little bit of extra money to help pay her way.

After leaving her cousin's house, she walked the short distance to the train station and caught the train back into Cardiff Queen Street station. She carefully stepped off the train and onto the platform. She looked up at the board, it was 6pm and her train was due at 6:15pm, so not long to wait she thought.

Standing waiting for the train, she noticed a couple further down on the other side of the platform, attempting what looked like a waltz, though clearly neither of them knew what they were doing.

At that moment Megan's train pulled up and the departed leaving Megan stood on the platform. Something had stopped her getting on the train.

She began to think, maybe she should go to the class and see what it was like, even if she just watched. Well she had missed her train, there was a bit of a wait until the next one and the Cardiff Bay train was due soon.

Before she could change her mind she hurried over to the other side of the platform, just as the Cardiff bay train arrived.

She couldn't quite fathom why she was doing this but something was telling her to give it a chance.

As she got off the train at Cardiff Bay, her legs were nervously jangling and her stomach was churning. Slowly she headed to the hall, which was only a short distance away.

At the hall she made her way, shakily inside. The door to the studio was ajar, light pouring out and several people rushed passed her. She moved closer, her jangling legs barely carrying her, until she was as close as she dared go.

Through the doorway in front of her the room was lined with a smooth, polished wooden floor and chairs at one side. There were several couples on the floor warming up, including the couple from the train station, who she had followed to the hall, as she hadn't known where the hall was, but had suspected that's where they were going and she was right.

The panic that had started when she had got off the train was intensifying. Thoughts of, everyone has got a partner and I can't go in there on my own filled her mind.

Just then the room fell silent and through the door she saw him, the instructor, move gracefully onto the floor, that was enough, she turned and fled the building and when she finally stopped to catch her breath, she was outside the train station.

How she had got there she didn't know, but her legs were like jelly, her heart was pounding and panic was set in. staggering into the station she climbed up onto her train and headed back to her granny's house.

CHAPTER THREE

The next day the sun was shining and granny was having her afternoon nap, so armed with a book, a drink and some of granny's homemade welsh cakes, Megan walked to her favourite spot, high up on the cliffs overlooking the heritage coast.

Once there she found a slightly shaded spot and spread out a blanket. She lay on the blanket, reading her book and relaxing.

A short while later she must have been so hooked in her book that she hadn't heard the footsteps approaching.
"Hello Megan"
She jumped, dropping the book and almost knocking her drink over. Steadying the bottle she looked up to see Caerwyn smiling down at her.

"What is it with you making me jump" she tried to hide a smile.

"I'm sorry, I didn't mean to, honest" he said with a teasing smile.

She composed herself then shuffled across the blanket and offered for him to sit down, which he did.

"So what are you doing here, I thought you would be delivering post?"

"It's my day off and I was on my way down to my favourite beach for a swim"

"Ah I see, well you have certainly got the weather for it"

"You are welcome to join me" he smiled.

"I really wish I could, but I can't, here is fine for me. Thank you for the offer though" she hurriedly replied.

She offered him one of granny's homemade welsh cakes in an effort to distract him, which he graciously accepted.

"These are delicious" he said but he couldn't help wondering why she couldn't go down to the beach. "Such a lovely spot this and the beach is not so easy to access so it makes it quieter which is great for a relaxing swim"

"It sure is. Do you know what else this spot is good for?"

"Go on then enlighten me"

"Peace and quiet to read a good book" she chuckled.

"Is that you trying to give me a hint" he winked at her. "Well I know when I'm not wanted!!"

"No, no I didn't mean it like that" then she noticed the cheeky grin on his face.

"It's ok, the sea is calling me for that swim. Sure I can't tempt you to join me?"

"No, I'm fine here but thanks anyway"

"No problem, see you later" he got up off the blanket and went to walk away but before he did he turned to look at her. "Oh and don't go thinking you can waltz off with one of those heroes in your book, they are not real you know" he winked, then left her too it.

As she sat there she couldn't help wondering about what he had said about waltzing off and if it meant something. He couldn't know about last night, could he? No he wasn't even there, it's just you over thinking things.

With the thoughts still in her mind, she got up to head back and packed up her things. Once ready she couldn't resist having a look down over the cliff wall to the beach below, well at Caerwyn to be precise!!

Stalking out of the sea, shorts dripping wet, he glanced up, just catching sight of Megan watching him before she turned away.

Again he found himself wondering why she couldn't come down. Something was troubling her, he knew the feeling, but he just couldn't fathom what. Whatever it was he had to tread carefully.

He dried and dressed, then climbed back up the path on the side of the cliff, hoping she would still be there at the top. When he got there he glanced around but she had already gone.

CHAPTER FOUR

The next day Megan went to get the post in from the post box and as she looked in, she noticed a hand written folded note, on top of the newspaper. She lifted it out and carefully opened it.

As she already suspected, it was from Caerwyn and read:

Megan
Sorry I missed you this morning.
I wanted to ask you if you would like to join me for a picnic today?
I will be at the same spot I found you at yesterday at 1pm with said picnic!!
Please save my waistline!!
I hope to see you there.
Caerwyn
P.S. If you do come, I am rather partial to your granny's homemade welsh cakes!!

"Have you got my newspaper there Megan?" her granny broke her thoughts.

"Yes, sorry I'm just getting it for you" flustered she shoved the note into her pocket and headed in with the newspaper.

"Ah thank you dear. So what have you got planned for today?" granny asked as she sat down in the chair with the newspaper.

"I don't know really, but it looks like lovely weather so I might take my book and go for a wander, if you don't mind that is?"

"No, not at all, you go, the fresh air will do you good"

"Thanks granny, wise words as always"

A while later, alone in her room she re read the note. She wanted to go, after all she still wondered if what he had said yesterday had meant something more than met the eye or if she was just over thinking things. But a part of he wondered if she should just stay away and concentrate on getting her life in order.

Sod it the weathers nice, I'm peckish and there's free food on offer, so why not live a little she said to herself, then gathered up her things, including a tin of granny's homemade welsh cakes and set off.

As she approached, she saw him, laid on a blanket, shirt off and a rucksack laid next to him. She stopped for a moment admiring the beauty of his shirtless body, glistening in the sun and then carefully crept up beside him.

"So this is what you posties do in your spare time is it?"

He jumped up, then when he saw who it was, he smiled "Nah only the ones who have got the body for it!!"

"Where are they then?!"

He chuckled "Watch it you. You found my note then"

"It would appear so. Thank you"

"You are very welcome. Now please say you brought some of your granny's homemade welsh cakes with you, I think you owe me after your earlier comment?!" he winked and chuckled.

"I sure did, though I'm not sure they are any good for your waistline anyway!!"

"Oh well who needs a waistline anyway!!"

He spread the picnic out and they ate and drank until they were stuffed.

"I'm glad you came"

"You mean your waistline is!!"

"No, well yes, but seriously I enjoy your company"

"That's good because I enjoy yours too"

They sat there looking at each other for a moment then looked away.

"Megan, I feel like I can talk to you and there's something that I want to share with you if that's ok with you?"

"Of course, I'm happy to listen so fire away"

"This isn't easy for me, I've never really spoken about this with anyone before but you seem different somehow, any way" he lifted his trouser leg to reveal scars on his knee.

She didn't speak, just looked and listened.

"I got these scars in my last year of school. The other kids used to pick on me as they thought I was gay because I love to dance. Ballroom and Latin dance is my passion, which apparently meant I must be gay.

That's where the waltz bit came from she thought to herself but remained silent, listening as he continued.

"One day I was walking down the stairs between classes and next thing I knew I was falling down the stairs. Some of the boys, who were picking on me, tripped me up, trying to put an end to my dancing.

Megan gasped in shock. How could people be so cruel she thought as she squeezed his hand gently.

I was taken to hospital and the head teacher and the police spoke to me about it but I just said it was an accident and left it at that. I didn't want any more trouble, after all I had enough to deal with as I couldn't dance with a dodgy knee and I didn't know if I would ever be able to again!!"

She noticed tears in his eyes as he spoke and silently put her hand back on his to comfort him.

"You don't have to continue if it is too painful, I understand" she whispered softly.

"I'm ok and I might as well continue as I have already got this far"

She squeezed his hand "If you are sure"

"After that I was quite lost for some time, until one day during my recovery, I flicked on the television and a Ballroom dance film was on. I didn't know if I wanted to watch it but I couldn't seem to turn it off. It was watching that film that reignited my passion and made me realise I wanted to dance again, after all if I gave up the bullies won and that wasn't right. So I did everything I could to get back into shape and got back on the dancefloor and now I do classes in Cardiff Bay.

Suddenly it clicked, she was right about his words yesterday meaning something. He must have seen her that night. "Sorry to interrupt you but I have to ask, you saw me the other night at that class in Cardiff Bay didn't you? That's what you meant when you said waltz yesterday?"

"It's ok and yes I did see you there"

She was puzzled. "But if you were there I would have recognised you, even in my state of panic, but you say you were there?"

"Well I should hope I was, as I am the instructor of the class, so it does help if I'm there!!"

"You are the instructor? How? The instructor didn't even have the same hair as you?!" she was confused.

"That's because I wear a wig, different clothing and I use a different name!!"

"That explains it but why?" before he could answer, it dawned on her. "You are still hiding from the bullies aren't you?" tears started to appear in her eyes.

"Yes. I didn't want them to win, but I can't face being bullied again, so I become a different person on the dancefloor to protect myself"

She was shocked, but yet understood, more than he knew.

"Anyway you know now and I feel like a weight has been lifted, so thank you for listening and I'm sorry about the tears, not very manly I know!!"

"No you have nothing to be sorry for. I'm glad you felt you could talk to me. I'm just sorry that you feel you have to hide your passion and I wish I could help" She squeezed his hand again and neither of them moved, they just there deep in thought and holding back the tears.

CHAPTER FIVE

"Buster, come here!!" a women shouted and brought them both out of their train of thought with a sudden jolt.

Looking down they noticed a dog sniffing round the empty welsh cake tin.

Megan leaned forward and stroked the dog. "You're too late buddy, he has eaten them all" she said looking at Caerwyn with a giggle.

"She helped too!!" he said looking between Megan and the dog with a cheeky grin.

The dog looked at them both then bounded off towards his owner while both, now composed, started clearing away the picnic.

"Do you know what I fancy doing now?" Caerwyn asked.

"Hmm go on then enlighten me?"

"Going for a dip in the sea, which is the perfect way to cool down. Would you care to join me?" he asked in the hope that she would feel more comfortable joining him.

"You don't know how much I want to join you, but I really can't, I'm sorry" she replied with an anxious look.

He thought for a moment, he wanted to help but he didn't want to push her or upset her, so he had to tread carefully. Just because he was ready to open up doesn't mean she is. "I'm a good listener if you would like to talk about anything or if there's anything I can help you with, I am happy to try" he asked carefully.

"Thank you, I really appreciate that"

She sat for a minute. Maybe I could open up a little and see how it goes she thought. Alright here goes.

"I haven't been down there since things changed and I'm not even sure I can get down there anymore even if I wanted to" she said while holding back the tears.

He could see she was struggling and squeezed her hand as she had with his. "It's ok, you don't have to tell me anything. I understand how difficult it is as I went through it myself, trying to get back down there after my accident, so you do what feels right for you. But if at any point you feel ready to try and get down there, I would be happy to help you and be there to support you every step of the way" he squeezed her hand again then he stood up and offered her a hand to get up.

"Thank you and thank you for being so understanding"

"You are very welcome. Perhaps we could do this again sometime soon?"

"I'd like that"

"Well I will no doubt see you on my post round, if not I will leave you another note in the post box!!" he winked at her with a cheeky grin.

"Great" she giggled. "Enjoy your dip"

"I will try" he said and smiled walking away towards the path that lead to the beach.

She watched him walking away but then suddenly she called out to him "Wait"

He turned sharply, a worried look on his face. "Is everything ok?" he shouted back worriedly.

"Yes, sorry that came out a bit sharper than I expected"

He walked towards her. "No need to apologise, you just startled me that's all"

"Sorry it's just I changed my mind, I would like to try and come with you, though I may not get very far, if that's ok with you that is?"

"Of course but are you sure you are ready?"

"No, but I'm as ready as I will ever be and as the saying goes, close your eyes and jump, though not literally obviously!!"

"I'm glad you cleared that up, as you had me worried there for a minute"

"Sorry I tend to witter when I'm nervous"

"It's ok I do the same. Well I'm ready if you are?"

"Yes let's do this" she replied.

As they set off towards the path he gently took her hand in his and he could feel her shaking nervously with each step.

Carefully, taking one step at a time they made their way down the path that wound down the side of the cliff to the beach below. Every so often they stopped to rest and take in the views. Each time they stopped he asked if she was ok and if she was sure she wanted to carry on and they kept going.

After a short while and plenty of stops they reached the bottom.

"There you go, we made it" he said gently.

Megan had been so distracted with nerves and the view that she didn't realise how far they had come in such a short space of time. She suddenly realised she was still holding his hand for dear life, released it and looked at him with tears in her eyes. "Thank you so much, I couldn't have done that without you and I'm sorry if I squeezed your hand to hard" she managed to say, still in shock at what she had just done and where she was.

"You are very welcome. I'm glad I could help and no you didn't squeeze my hand too hard at all" he replied while helping her to sit down on a rock to rest and gather her thoughts.

"I'd forgotten how beautiful and quiet it is down here. It brings back memories of many days spent down here with my dad, a net and a bucket!!"

He looked at her puzzled. "I can understand your dad being down here but what was the net and bucket for?" he asked.

She laughed "Sorry, let me elaborate. When we were kids, my sister and I used to come down here most school holidays and my dad and I used to love coming down here prawning.

We left my mum and my sister on Southerndown beach as neither of them had heads for heights. We walked along this beach and went home with buckets of prawns to eat as well as the occasional crab, though my dad normally used the crabs for fishing bait. Along the way we competed to see how many golf balls we could find, that had strayed from the golf course on the cliffs above!!

We were even lucky enough to catch two lobsters in the net on two different occasions" she told him with tears in her eyes.

"That sounds amazing, I wish I could do that but I wouldn't know where to start, though I'm guessing with a net and bucket?!" he laughed and winked at her.

She laughed "That's as good a place as any to start"

She looked around at the view. "You know there are so many things I would love to be able to do that I used to do"

"Like what?"

"Ballroom dancing and coming down here"

"Well you have made it down here"

"True but I just hope I can get back up the path again"

"Don't worry we will do it together and I will be there every step of the way" he reassured her.

"Thank you. You are so kind"

"It's nothing really, I know how you feel, have been where you are and I just want to help you" he said squeezing her hand.

"Thank you, I really appreciate your help and support. I just wish there was something I could do to help you in return"

"Well you have already been an excellent listener"

"I suppose there is that"

They both sat looking out to sea, deep in thought.

"You know I've just had an idea of how we can help each other out" Caerwyn suddenly said bringing them both out of their trains of thought.

"Hmm that sounds ominous but go on then what's the idea?" she looked at him inquisitively.

"Well I quite fancy learning prawning, you would like to learn ballroom dancing and we have the perfect space right here to do both. So we could do a deal, you teach me prawning and I will teach you Ballroom dancing. What do you think?"

"Well I hate to state the obvious but there is no dance floor and we haven't got a net and bucket?!" she exclaimed.

"We can use the sand as our dance floor and I will get a net and bucket to bring with us next time"

"Got it all planned out haven't you!!"

"Well it's only an idea"

"Well I think it is a great idea, but there is something you should know" she looked anxiously at him.

"It's ok, you don't have to tell me" he smiled.

She stared at the view, holding back tears and saw him watching her with a look of kindness and care in his eyes. In that moment she knew she wanted to open up to him.

CHAPTER SIX

"I was 15 years old when it all started. It was one evening and I had been lying on my bed watching my favourite chef's new cookery series on the television when I just happened to look at my feet and I thought I'm sure my big toe on my left foot is swollen but was I imagining it as quite often the light can play tricks on me, I wasn't sure but I didn't want to miss the end of my program, typical me, so I decided to watch it and then ask my mum and dad for their opinion on my toe.

Once my program had finished I checked again and it still looked swollen, so I went downstairs to the living room where my mum and dad were sitting watching the television and showed them my toe and they both agreed it was swollen and needed to be looked at by a doctor.

That's when I started to worry but I knew they were right and if nothing else it would put our minds at rest or so we thought. So after that night I went to see the doctor and so began the longest year spent looking for answers or at least it felt like that.

During that long year we saw GP's, Physiotherapists and Podiatric specialists also known as foot Doctors and none of them knew what was wrong, although there was a glimmer of hope when a Physiotherapist put an ultrasound machine on my toe and I felt sharp pains in my toe which apparently meant there was something definitely wrong with it, but the only thing we could come up with was an injury from step aerobics in physical education class at school.

We were all at our wits end and were fast losing hope of finding an answer me especially. In my mind it was like a jigsaw puzzle, which normally I enjoy doing, but this one had the vital piece missing and it seemed like it didn't want to be found, which as I already had obsessive compulsive disorder, didn't bode well.

I remember feeling worried and scared but I knew I had to be strong and hide how I really felt for my family and friends sake as I didn't want them to worry about me when they had got their own lives to live.

But there was one day in particular, when I began to realise how others were feeling about this situation.

It was late summer and my parents, my younger sister and I were staying here with my Granny. It was a lovely sunny day and my dad and I decided to do one of our favourite things blackberry picking, mum was not very impressed as she had to think of ways to cook them and then wash and cook them when we returned, that never stopped us but on the other hand it kept us happy and out from under her feet so that made up for it.

So off we went, armed with a box to put the blackberries in, to a spot we found with several blackberry bushes on the side of a small hill, overlooking the river. We climbed up to the bushes and I held the box whilst dad filled it with the lovely, juicy blackberries. I always let dad do the picking so he can get prickled and covered in juice as I am not as daft as he is!!!!

As I stood there, I felt a dull ache in my big toe and I noticed how it was becoming more difficult and painful to do things that I enjoyed. My dad and I started talking about the situation and he said that he hoped we could find out what was wrong with me and hopefully get it treated. I could see in his eyes that he was worried but he wasn't going to let on that he was because being a typical man and father, he was determined to be strong for me and everyone else. We both said we hoped it wasn't going to be anything serious that could stop me living a normal life or even result in me being in a wheelchair as I love walking and being active and didn't want to lose the ability to do the things I enjoy doing but In my mind I knew that things were going to change and that they would probably never be the same again.

Stood on the side of that hill, in the warm sunshine, holding onto the box that was slowly being filled with blackberries, I could feel myself holding back the tears in my eyes afraid that if even one tiny drop should escape my fears would be shown and the tears wouldn't stop. I was so scared of what the future would hold and even more scared of showing or saying how I really felt.

It was in that moment that I became determined to find out what was wrong with me and whether it could be treated or even cured"

She stopped, took a deep breath and looked into the distance, still holding back the tears.

He didn't say a word, instead he took her hand in his and gently squeezed it to let her know he was there.
After a few moments she continued.

"Almost a year had gone by and still no answers had been found and the jigsaw puzzle was still missing the vital piece. By this time I had lost all my energy and hope and I was sure everyone else had too. It was then that fate intervened, well alright maybe not fate but my body or my right foot to be precise. I had woken one morning to find that two of my toes on my right foot had become swollen, which at first we thought was an ingrowing toenail but it turned out to be the key to the missing part of the jigsaw puzzle. With this new found pain and swelling came a renewal of our hope and for me some relief that all was not lost.

It was then that things happened quite quickly. I went to see the Podiatric specialist or foot Doctor for the umpteenth time, I'm sure he must have been fed up of me by then and he decided to refer me to a Rheumatology specialist or Arthritis Consultant at the hospital as he suspected it was either gout or arthritis.

Finally we were getting somewhere, however it could be several months before I could get an appointment and as we had already waited this long we decided that there was only one thing for it, we would have to go privately, which meant we would have to pay but we could get an appointment much quicker so it would be worth it. So we booked an appointment and my parents agreed to pay for it, for which I am very grateful and will never forget what they did for me.

In the run up to the appointment my nerves were all over the place and worry set in, which didn't help when I was supposed to be revising for my GCSE exams and all I could do was hope and watch my family and friends trying to hide their worry.

As the day of the appointment dawned, my nerves were all over the place and all sorts of feelings and emotions were building inside me. My mum and I got in the car and off we went to the hospital. When we got there we waited in the waiting room, which was well presented which is what you would expect for a private hospital. But sat in that waiting room, with people bustling about, all I could think of was what the consultant might say and would he have the answers we all wanted.

After what seemed like ages but was actually only a few minutes, the consultant came out of his consulting room and called my name and I froze for a split second. As we stood up and walked towards the room, panic, worry and nerves set in.

He welcomed us in and asked us to take a seat. He then went over everything that happened, examined me and did various tests. Then came the dreaded diagnosis. The room was silent, I was struggling to control my nerves and I was holding my breath for what seemed like ages but was actually only a second or two. What happened next was a bit of a blur. He told me I have got Juvenile Idiopathic Arthritis."

Megan looked up at Caerwyn, his eyes filled with tears and shock and she felt him squeeze her hand tightly. She knew he didn't have the words just then so she carried on and as she did a tear escaped and slid down her cheek.

"I sat there in shock, I was relieved that we knew what it was but at the same tine scared of what it meant and what was going to happen next. The hardest bit was when he told me there was no cure for arthritis but with it being Juvenile there was a chance it may cure itself, there were no guarantees though, which if I wasn't in shock, might have given me some hope but at that stage my mind just wasn't taking anything in. He went on to tell us what would happen next, I could hear what he was saying, but I wasn't taking any of it in, all I wanted was to get out of that room and to try and get my head straight.

Once he had finished explaining everything we got up, thanked him and slowly walked out of the room. Mum went and paid the bill at the reception desk and then we headed for the exit doors.

We walked out of the doors and both stopped just outside to take a minute and mum asked me if I was alright and if I had understood what had been said. I didn't know what to say so I just said yes and carried on to the car as I didn't feel like talking at that moment.

The journey home was quiet, I don't think either of us really knew what to say and we were both in shock. As we drove down the road, the fields on either side flying past the window and the village where we live in, in the distance getting closer and closer, all I could think of was I wanted to tell my best friend as I knew he would be waiting to know what happened and I hoped he would give me some comfort and wise words.

With my hands shaking and my thoughts all over the place I fished my mobile phone out of my pocket and dialled my best friends number and waited for him to answer but I didn't know what I was going to say. At that moment he answered the phone and I found myself desperately trying to hold back the tears as I tried to explain what had happened but despite my best efforts the tears started flowing. He gave me some comfort and wise words and said he would come and see me later that day after he finished work.

After that day things were never the same, we were all relieved to know what was wrong with me but at the same time we were all trying to deal with the shock and what was going to happen next in our own ways."

She was really struggling to hold back the tears now but determination willed her on.

"I spent the next few months going backwards and forwards to the hospital for various tests and appointments and was put on weekly medication injections so I was starting to feel like a pin cushion but on the positive side I had been transferred on to the main hospital so my parents didn't have to pay for private treatment and of course all the tests were helping the consultant treat my condition so it wasn't all bad. Gradually I began to feel like I was getting my head around everything and that things were getting easier. I was in the middle of my exams at school when I was diagnosed so that didn't help but I managed to get through them and get the grades to go to college.

Three months later I started at college but it seemed it wasn't to be as my condition dealt me another blow as my right knee became swollen and painful. My mind went into overdrive again with worry as I could barely walk and I didn't know how I was going to cope. We went back to the hospital and were told the arthritis had now spread to my right knee, so I had got it in both of my feet and my right knee. I found myself thinking where is it going to appear next.

That was the start of a long year. As I could barely walk, I was pretty much house bound for a year. However as much as I wanted to give up, my parents wouldn't let me and they encouraged me to look into home learning courses that I could do while I couldn't get out of the house. So I completed a computer course and got a good grade which helped to keep my brain going and to some degree helped to take my mind off the arthritis but it still sits in the back of your mind and the slightest thing can set it off again.

When I wasn't busy doing my course, my mum and her best friend took me out in the car shopping and more often than not that included breakfast or lunch. It was good to get out of the house and I always enjoyed the company and the food!! But it came at a price the food and the shopping!! But seriously the highest price was the struggle I faced every time I got in or out of the car, as at that stage I was in a lot of pain and had a lot of swelling in my feet as well as my knee which meant I couldn't bend it.

So every time I got in the car I had to sit sideways on the back seat of the car with my legs and feet hanging out of the door and then lie across the back seats, gently pull my legs across the seats whilst holding onto my knee and try and sit up and somehow pull my leg round and down which wasn't easy with the limited space so I would end up facing the front and I could then put my seatbelt on and to get out of the car it was the same procedure but the opposite way. All this was done whilst being in a lot of pain physically and mentally.

I dreaded getting in and out of the car, not just because of the pain, that I could deal with to some degree, but it was the feeling of embarrassment, that I was slowing people down and most of all I hated it that the people I love and care about had to watch me struggle with such a simple task and that's what I dreaded the most. I knew they were only trying to help me live my life and get out and about, for which I was very grateful for, but I could see in their eyes that like me they were struggling with the situation but neither I nor they, would dare admit it as we were all trying to be strong for one and other.

Once I had got out of the car the next struggle I faced was walking as I could barely put one foot in front of the other never mind trying to co-ordinate which way they were going, most of the time I think one foot wanted to go for breakfast and the other foot wanted to go for lunch!!!!

But anyway I managed to walk all be it very slowly, with a limp and with the help of being on the arm of at least one person unless there were three of us and then I was on the arms of one either side of me. This was a great support and meant that even though I couldn't walk very far I could at least stretch my legs a little to avoid them getting too stiff and get out of the house.

Apart from the occasional trip out, I spent most of my time in the house which is where I faced one of the hardest challenges I have ever had to face. I woke up one morning and as I lay in bed I realised I couldn't move. The tears started to flow, fear and panic set in and even though I didn't want it I knew I needed help, so I shouted out to my mum and dad who were if not in the kitchen below then were somewhere in the house.

Almost immediately they came racing up the stairs like a herd of elephants and they were shouting to ask me what was wrong but I just couldn't find the words to reply. My bedroom door flew open and the rushed in coming to a panicked halt at the side of my bed. They then asked me what was wrong and with tears streaming down my face I exclaimed that I couldn't move.

As I lay there helpless they gradually moved my legs round the bed and over the side and then carefully lifted me round to a seated position on the edge of my bed. Then they lifted me up off my bed, from there with them supporting me at both sides, I was able to shuffle gradually along the corridor to the stairs, from there we decided the easiest way to do it, was to do as I had done many times as a child and slide down one flight of stairs then drag myself up the other flight of stairs on the opposite side on my bottom. So they carefully helped me down onto the first step and then I did the rest whilst they stood and watched in case I needed any help.

After what seemed like ages I made it to the top of the second flight of stairs, where they helped me up onto my feet and into the bathroom and then once I had somehow managed to use the bathroom, we did the same procedure back to my bedroom.

Once I was back in my bedroom, sitting on the edge of my bed I found I had regained some movement so I decided to try and get dressed. My mum passed me my clothes, the top half was easy enough but then came the bottom half from the waist down. I tried and tried but with tears in my eyes I knew I couldn't do it and at that moment fear and rage took over and I launched, the sock I had been trying to put on, at my bedroom wall narrowly missing my mum in the process, at that stage my dad had left the room having decided the dressing part wasn't for him.

At that moment I could feel the tears burning my eyes with fear and anger running through me because I couldn't dress myself properly so I lay back and cried into my pillow with my mum trying to comfort me and offer me help but somehow the words it will be ok and let me help you didn't bring me any comfort at that moment. I felt useless, that my independence had been taken away from me and I just wanted to give up.

Eventually I knew I had to give in and except help as I couldn't stay in bed all day, as I am the sort of person that likes to be up and about doing things however difficult that might be. Reluctantly I let my mum dress me from the waist down.

After that I continued on with the day as best as I could. Gradually I became able to move properly again and get on with things as best I could."

Megan and Caerwyn looked at each other again, both struggling with the tears and she carried on, afraid to stop as she knew she wouldn't be able to carry on.

"As I struggled on Christmas came and I found the strength to make it down the road and round the corner to the village duck pond to the lights on the tree in the middle of the pond being switched on and then home again. It was that night, when my mum got home that she told me she had bumped into an old friend of mine and he had said just because I have got arthritis on the outside I am still the same person I have always been on the inside and these words have stayed with me ever since and continue to bring some comfort.

After nearly a year of being practically house bound, the weekly medication injections I was on started damaging my liver and after spending a week in hospital so they could monitor my arthritis as it wasn't improving very well, the consultant decided to try putting me on a new medication. I had gone from just a pin cushion to a guinea pig and a pin cushion now but as I could barely walk anything was worth a try but nothing could prepare us for what happened next.

It was the day of my first injection of the new medication and I limped through the hospital doors into the waiting room, told the receptionist I was there and then carefully sat in the nearest available seat in the waiting room.

As I sat there all I could think of was how much would this injection hurt well alright I was also thinking would it actually do anything to help me.

At that moment the specialist nurse who administers and checks medications called me in and after explaining everything, administered the injection, which was a bit painful, who had the idea of putting lemon juice well citric acid in to preserve it I don't know but I think it is better suited to a gin and tonic or a pancake!!!! Anyway I would get used to the pain so once everything was sorted I limped out of the hospital and we headed home.

The following morning I awoke to rather a shock. I carefully climbed out of bed as usual and stood up, was I imagining it, I wasn't sure so I opened the bedroom door and started walking faster and faster until I was almost running across the corridor, well alright let's not overdo it but I could move without limping and with very little pain. I shouted out to mum and dad and mum started panicking as per usual but I exclaimed that I could walk without limping and then I proceeded to show them. They too were shocked and couldn't believe their eyes.

Once the initial shock wore off we all realised we weren't imagining it, for the first time in two and a half years there was some joy and a new hope that I could live a normal life doing the things I enjoy. I could see the struggle in their eyes had turned to joy and hope and as for me well I was always going to be worried about what was going to happen next but for once I was happy and more hopeful about the future.

As the days went on I continued to feel better and started to live my life again.

But although physically I was feeling better and stronger, I began to realise that it had been covering up what was really going on mentally, as depression and anxiety started to show through.

After that I started to struggle mentally with the depression and anxiety causing me to have a mental breakdown where I felt like someone else had taken over my body like it wasn't me and I couldn't think straight, I didn't know what I was doing, I just kept crying and ran off as I just didn't want to be near anyone.

Eventually I came out of it and calmed myself down. After that I continued having what I would call mini breakdowns and one big one but not as bad as the first one.

It was then that I knew I needed help so I went to see the doctor who then referred me to see a counsellor. To this I had the same thoughts many other people have, how on earth was talking about it going to help but although I was sceptical I gave it a go and to my surprise it did help. Each time I went I found it easier to talk to someone who was neutral to the situation and then when I left it felt like a weight had been lifted off my mind and I felt like things were easier to cope with. After so many sessions it was time for me to go it alone with the help of some very useful coping techniques.

Apart from talking to people the one tip that I did find helped was the worry tree which consisted of a tree like diagram which had a number of questions attached. The questions started with what is worrying you then when you had worked that out, the next question was what could you do to sort out what was worrying you. Then you had to work out whether you could do anything straight away and if you could then do it and that should stop the worry.

On the other hand if you couldn't do anything about it straight away then plan what you are going to do about it and when you are going to do it then find something you enjoy doing for example reading a book, baking a cake or watching the TV, so you can put what you are worrying about to one side and to take your mind off what you were worrying about until it's the time to deal with what was worrying you. I like most people sceptical about this method but I found it really does work and helps to stop the worrying.

Finally I was coping physically and mentally and the consultant had after gradually reducing the medication finally taken me off it altogether. But then not long after fate dealt another blow or rather a car hitting the back of my car causing a minor accident. At the time I was fine apart from a bit of shock, but little did I know what was to come.

After the accident I began to ache a bit and then all of a sudden I started getting pain in my backside and no it wasn't my parents or my little sister!! It was my pelvis and it was getting so bad I could barely walk and then one morning I woke up and I tried to put my socks on, I couldn't do it, I could feel the tears stinging my eyes and the anger built up inside me until I couldn't contain it any longer and I grabbed the socks and threw them across the room.

Why was this happening again, it was like I had gone back several years and all I could think was is this what it is going to be like for the rest of my life, having no independence, having to be cared for and maybe even be in a wheelchair not being able to walk and although I knew there were people a lot worse off than me, I was so angry and scared that it didn't occur to me at the time. I just lay on the bed crying and I just wanted to give up. I had got through this once already and I didn't think I had the strength to get through it again.

But with a lot of help and support from my family and friends I found the strength to carry on and see the consultant which I knew that it meant that after only a year off the medication I would have to go back on it and I was right the consultant did put me back on it, but on the positive side it helped me feel better.

After years of emotional and physical struggles and a failed second attempt to come of the medication, I am finally living an almost normal life and although the arthritis is never far from my mind and every day I wonder what my arthritis will do next, I know that I have family and friends who are always there to help and support me and I hope that one day I might even be able to come off the medication injections again this time for good.

But for now I am living my life as normal as I can and when I look in my family and friends eyes the sadness and worry has almost gone and I see joy, happiness and hope for the future ahead which gives me the strength to continue on with my life."

Megan and Caerwyn sat there looking at each other, tears flowing down both their faces and neither able to speak. Without a word Caerwyn gently let go of Megan's hand, opened his arms and Megan moved slowly into them. He wrapped his arms around her and squeezed her softly so she knew he was there for her.

CHAPTER SEVEN

A sudden swish at their feet brought them out of their daze with a start and Megan jumped not realising what it was.

"It's ok, it's just the sea, the tide has started coming in, that said we should probably start heading back up, or else we will be needing the coastguard!!" he exclaimed with a giggle.

Wiping away the tears with a tissue from her pocket, she smiled. "That seems like a wise idea, the going back up, though using the coastguard when necessary is wise too"

"Agreed" he said going to get up with a struggle.

"Are you ok?" she asked worriedly.

"Yes fine, just sitting for too long gets me a little stiff but I will be fine once we start moving"

"I know that feeling"

Before he could get fully up she caught his hand and looked at him. "Thank you"

"What for?"

"For listening, not judging me and for not running a mile after me telling you all that and I'm sorry I went on a bit but once I started I couldn't stop"

"I'm so glad you felt able to open up to me about what you went through and I really appreciate you listening to me too. Rest assured I'm not about to go anywhere, well except up the cliff to get us both home safely!!"

She smiled.

"Honestly Megan I understand what you are going through. I'm glad we are able to talk about things as I believe talking does help, we are lucky we have found each other and through friendship been able to open up to each other. I really value our friendship and hope that we can continue to help each other" he said squeezing her hand.

"That really means a lot, thank you and I really value our friendship too.

Another wave lapped at their feet.

"I think the sea is trying to tell us something!!" he winked at her.

She laughed "Quite right it is too!!"

He helped her up onto her feet and they gathered up their belongings. They set off towards the steps but after only a short distance she stopped and pointed towards a rock pool. "Look a prawn!!" she exclaimed pointing at it so he could see where she was looking.

"Oh wow that's amazing. It looks nothing like the ones you get in the shops!!"

She laughed. "No silly it has got its shell on and cooked ones are pink while raw ones are grey!! Plus they look different in their natural habitat"

"I know the difference between cooked and raw prawns" he laughed. "But I've never seen one in the wild before. They are amazing to watch"

"Not so easy to catch though!!" she laughed.

"Does that mean you are going to teach me?" he asked with his best hopeful eyes.

"Hmm I guess we can give it a go, though I am a little bit rusty and you will have to remember to bring a strong net and bucket"

"You don't look rusty!!" he said with a cheeky grin.

"Oi cheeky, I can still change my mind you know"

"Sorry I couldn't resist. I appreciate you agreeing to teach me, I will look forward to it and to teaching you to dance. Oh and I will call at the fishing tackle shop and get the strongest net and bucket they have" he smiled.

"Alright don't lay it on too thick!!"

The both laughed and set off again. Pausing at the start of the uphill path he turned to her and held out his hand "Ready?"

"As I will ever be"

"Don't worry we will take it one step at a time and rest when we need to"

"Ok let's do it" she grabbed his hand and up they climbed.

They carefully climbed up the path leading up the side of the cliff, stopping every so often for them both to have a rest and enjoy the spectacular views.

After a short while they reached the top and paused to look at the view and to take in the path they had just climbed. Neither of them said a word, just took in the view while they caught their breaths.

Caerwyn turned to Megan and gently squeezed her hand "You did it" he smiled.

"I did" she said tears welling up in her eyes.

He carefully released his hand from hers and gently put his arm around her shoulders. "I am so pleased for you, I know that wasn't easy, I mean it's a struggle for me too but it felt so much easier knowing I wasn't alone and knowing how much doing that climb meant to you, I'm so glad I was able to help you get your wish to come true"

She smiled, wiping away the tears from her eyes. Thank you so much. I didn't think I would ever be able to do that again but you proved me wrong. I couldn't have done it without you. You really are a true friend and your support and friendship is invaluable to me. I really appreciate it.

"You are so very welcome and yours is to me too"

They smiled at each other and neither moved.

"Anyway" she said suddenly realising she was staring at him and not wanting to appear rude.

"Yes anyway I guess we ought to be heading home"

"That sounds like a good idea"

"Speaking of ideas, when shall we start our lessons?" he winked at her.

"You make it sound like we are at school" she giggled.

"No this is much better than school and you don't get views or company like this at school" he laughed.

"That's very true though the lads are better at school"

"Oh charming"

"I'm only joking"

"That's ok then I will let you off"

"We appear to have digressed a bit"

"True very true, so when is our first session to be?"

"Alright steady on, now you've gone from school to something that could be misconstrued as naughty!!" she laughed.

He covered his eyes and tried not to laugh. to not much success.

"Let's call it a class"

"Isn't that something you drink out of?!" he said with a puzzled look

"No that's a glass and I said class" she said exasperatedly.

He laughed and gave her a cheeky grin.

Realising he was joking she laughed. "For goodness sake we are getting nowhere fast here"

"Yes you are right, all joking aside, I am working tomorrow then I've got the weekend off so how about we meet here on Friday at 1pm, that will give me chance to nip to the fishing tackle shop for that net and bucket in the morning?"

"That sounds perfect"

"Great. I will bring the net and bucket and you can bring the picnic. Oh and don't forget the welsh cakes!!" he winked cheekily.

"Ok deal. You and welsh cakes!!" she laughed.

"Your gran makes the best welsh cakes ever so how can I not indulge now and then, besides a little of what you fancy does you good!!"

"Ok I guess you have a point" she laughed.

"Yep so I can have welsh cakes then?" he said with a cheeky wink.

"Go on then seeing as you have been so helpful"

"Thank you. Anyway I better let you get home, see you Friday"

"Yes see you Friday"

CHAPTER EIGHT

Friday came quite quickly. Megan hadn't seen Caerwyn on his round the day before as she had been out shopping for her granny, but today she was going to. She was nervous and excited at the same time, which seemed silly as she was only going to meet a friend. Oh for goodness sake pull yourself together Megan she said to herself.

She carefully filled her rucksack with the requested picnic, consisting of sandwiches, crisps, some fruit, a couple of bottles of diluted juice and a tin of the promised welsh cakes.

Megan had also dug out the photo from her dancing days to show him but she wasn't sure about that so put it in her pocket and would decide when she saw him.

A short while later Megan arrived at their meeting place. She was a little early and Caerwyn wasn't there yet, that didn't matter though as she enjoyed looking at the view and taking in the noises around her.

A fishing boat caught her eye out on the sea and she watched as it bobbed steadily across the waves, with fishing rods sticking out of the back of the boat. She wondered what they were catching out there and then she found herself thinking about whether Caerwyn would like prawning and if they would be able to net any. Oh I'm sure he will do just fine she thought and at that moment, as if his ears had been burning, he appeared behind her.

"Hi"

"Hi"

"I see you brought the picnic"

"I sure did and you've got the net and bucket"

"Looks like we are all set then, shall we go?"

"Um you might want to look over the wall first!!"

He moved to stand next to her and looked over the wall. "Oh I see what you mean, that tide needs to be out a bit further before we can get down there. Oh well, why don't we have our picnic up here first, then by the time we have eaten, the tide should have gone out a bit. Plus we will be able to walk off our food on the way down, there's nothing worse than dancing on a full stomach!!"

"Sounds like a plan and you are quite right about dancing on a full stomach!!" she said slightly apprehensive about the dancing.

They laid out the blanket and food then sat down on either side of the blanket.

"So are you ready to dance again?"

"Are you ready to learn how to net prawns?"

"I asked first" he said with a cheeky grin.

"I don't know, I mean I'm not sure it's such a good idea. What if I fall or make a fool of myself?" she said nervously.

"You love dancing right? Plus you've got me as your teacher what could possibly go wrong?!" He winked. "But in all seriousness, I can tell you are passionate about ballroom and Latin dance, just like I am and I promise I will do my best not to let you fall or make a fool of yourself. We have both got ailments but that shouldn't stop us doing what we are passionate about and helping each other achieve that, besides there will only be the two of us and the odd passer-by down there so whatever happens we will deal with it together because that's what friends are for"

"Thank you I really appreciate that"

"You are very welcome and it's all true but if you really don't feel ready then I completely understand, the decision is yours"

"You make it sound so easy and you know what you are right, perhaps I can be the girl in the photo again, though a little bit older!!"

He was puzzled until she carefully took the photo out of her pocket and showed him. The photo was of her in a dress and dance shoes.

"That was taken during my dance exams"

"You look stunning and so happy, you can see the passion in your eyes"

"Thank you. I was happy then before the arthritis took it all away from me" she said holding back a tear.

"Hey you mustn't let the arthritis hold you back, you just have to adapt a bit and if you will allow me to help you, I'm sure I can get you dancing again"

"You are right as always and you know what let's do it!!"

"Great and don't worry I will be there every step of the way"

"Thank you" she smiled,

"Hey have you still got that dress and those shoes?"

"Sadly not. I don't know what happened to them but I doubt they would fit now anyway!! I did love those shoes, I even thought about buying another pair but it seemed pointless and an unnecessary expense, as for the dress, it was lovely but I always wanted a purple Latin dance dress and we couldn't find a cheap enough one so I settled for that dress instead"

"Well I think they look great on you and who knows, maybe you could still get another pair of shoes and that purple dress!!"

"Let's not get ahead of ourselves, I don't even know if I can dance let alone wear a pair of shoes like that again!!"

"Well there's only one way to find out!!"

They sat and ate their food as slowly the tide started to go out below them. Once they had finished they packed everything away and helped each other scramble to their feet.

Caerwyn peered over the wall. "The tide looks to be heading in the right direction, it should be out far enough when we get down there"

Megan joined him next to the small stone wall at the edge of the cliff. "It sure is. Just look at that view, the cliffs with their natural erosion, the sand, the sea and the rock ledges all along the beach for miles are amazing!!"

"It really is spectacular and very romantic!!" he said with a cheeky grin.

"Less of that!! Now come on we've got work to do"

"Yes miss!!" he laughed.

He set off but she stopped him in his tracks. "Hmm Caerwyn aren't you forgetting something?"

"Well come on, what are you waiting for?"

"No not me" she said looking towards the net and bucket propped up against the wall.

"Oh yes we need those!!" he said cheekily as he went to pick them up.

"Well they would be more use for prawning than propping a wall up!!" she laughed.

"That's very true and we better get a move on or else that tide will be back in before we get down there"

"Good point, let's go"

After a short while they made it to the bottom of the cliff.

"Right what shall we do first?"

"Prawning I think, stretch our legs and finish walking our food off"

"Good idea, lead on miss"

"Right first we need a big rock pool and don't forget to look for stray golf balls!! Oh and…."

Before she could say it he slid on a piece of wet seaweed.

"Well I was going to say be careful on the wet, slimy, green seaweed as it is very slippery but you just worked that one out for yourself!!" she said trying not to laugh.

"Yes, that will teach me for not watching where my feet are going. Note to self I'm not on a dancefloor now so do watch where feet are going!!"

"I hadn't thought of that but you are right and are you ok?"

"Aren't I always" he laughed "I'm fine thank you"

"Hmm that's debatable. Anyway here's a good looking rock pool"

"I can't see the appeal myself!!" They both laughed.

"Will you please concentrate"

"Yes miss, sorry miss!!"

"Right get your net and run it along under the ledge like this" she ran the net under the ledge. "Oh and be careful so you don't snag the net. Here you try" she handed him the net.

He followed her instructions and then lifted the net out, swung it round to show her and narrowly missed her.

"Whoa careful you nearly had me over then!!"

"I'm so sorry. I got a bit over excited at what was in the net and forgot how long the net is!!" he said apologetically.

"It's ok, no harm done, just go steady. It's a good job granny is not with us or she would have said"

"You are like a bull in a china shop!!" they both said in unison and then laughed.

"I will do"

"Good now what were you going to show me in the net?"

"Oh yes, look prawns, should we put them in the bucket?"

"No they are only small so we put those ones back. We only take the big ones as they are easier to handle"

"Right" he said and put them back.

They carried on going from rock pool to rock pool but there were only small prawns about.

After a while she stopped and bent down trying to get a golf ball that was wedged between the rocks.

"What have you found?" he said coming to stand beside her.

"A golf ball, I was hoping to get it out and claim it before you saw it, but it is stuck!!"

"Oh that's how it is, is it?" he laughed. "Here let me try"

What she didn't tell him was she had managed to loosen it a bit so when he knelt down and tried it suddenly pinged out, knocking him of balance and bounced across the rocks. She stood watching and trying not to laugh as he was now sitting in a shallow rock pool!!"

He looked at her. "You knew that was going to happen didn't you?!"

"Well I knew it was loose but I didn't expect that to happen!!" she gave him a hand to get up.

"Hmm" he said as he walked across the rocks to retrieve it, "Well I guess I will let you have that one then but I am having this one!!"

"Hang on a minute where did that one come from" she looked at him puzzled.

"This one you found led me to it" he laughed.

"Oh bother, well I guess that makes us even on the golf ball hunt, for now!!"

He smiled and they turned back the way they came. "Time to head back and see if we can find your dancing feet!!"

"Ok let's go"

They carefully made their way back checking a few rock pools they had missed as they went. Unfortunately the big prawns were hiding and they didn't find any more stray golf balls either, so they called it a draw and hoped for better luck next time.

They made it back to the little sandy patch by the path they had climbed down earlier and put their things on a rock, well away from the tide.

"So are you ready?" he asked.

"Are you sure we can dance here, there's no dancefloor or music to dance too?"

"Ah but that is where you are wrong. The sand is our dancefloor and the sea is our music. Take your shoes off, listen and feel" he said as he took his own shoes and socks off.

She took her shoes and socks off and listened to the waves rolling across the sea and breaking over the sand. She felt the sand beneath her feet, soft and warm. Then without a sound she placed her hand in the hand he had extended to her and together they glided effortlessly across the sand, turning every so often.

After a while she realised they had stopped and he was watching her.

"You see, you just danced a waltz to the sounds of the sea"

"Wow, I can't believe it. That was enchanting and I danced for the first time since everything changed" she manged to say with shock, happiness and tears in her eyes.

"You did and very beautifully too" he smiled.

"Thank you so much" she said wiping the tears away from her eyes.

"You are very welcome and you see you don't need shiny floors and music to dance, you can dance anywhere"

"It would appear you can and I didn't make a fool of myself, well at least I don't think I did?"

"No not at all because you weren't thinking you just went with the flow, which is what dancing is all about"

"It sure is"

"Oh crumbs the tide is after us again, we better get moving"

They quickly put their shoes and socks back on, gathered up their belongings and headed slowly up the side of the cliff.

When they reached the top they paused to catch their breaths.

"Thank you for today, I have really enjoyed it, even though our bucket is empty, except for two golf balls and my backside is a little damp!!" he laughed.

She laughed. "I've really enjoyed it too and thank you so much for helping me to dance again"

"No problem, I'm glad to be of service and as they say until next time or in our case Sunday if you are free?"

"Yes I'm free, I will look forward to it and hopefully you will stay upright!!"

"I will certainly try!! Same time, same place?"

"Of course"

"Great and don't forget the…."

"Welsh cakes!!" they both said in unison and laughed.

"How did you know?"

"Intuition" she laughed.

"Predictability more like!!"

"Exactly. See you on Sunday and thanks again" she smiled.

"No problem, see you on Sunday and thank you too" he smiled back.

CHAPTER NINE

The following Sunday Megan and Caerwyn met up again, had their picnic then went prawning but again the prawns were hiding and there wasn't even a golf ball to be found. They didn't let that dampen their spirits though and turned their attention to the dancing.

"What's your favourite dance?" he asked.
"The jive, I remember flying around the dancefloor and the feeling of forgetting everything around you and it was almost like you were going to take off, it was an amazing feeling. What's your favourite dance?"
"Mines the rumba because it's slow, sensual, emotive and beautiful to watch and dance"
"Not so good for hiding mistakes though!!"
"That's true, though if the story is captivating enough the audience shouldn't notice any mistakes"

"That's true"
"Hey how about we try a jive today, ladies first, then a rumba on my next day off, which is Thursday, if you are free?"
"That sounds good and yes I am available on Thursday but I'm not sure sand is suitable for a fast dance, is it?"
"Great and of course it is, come here and I will prove it" he smiled cheekily and held his hand out.
She took his hand and he went over the basic steps for a jive to refresh her memory and they danced, kicks, flicks, chasse's and turns, fast and fluid until they could dance no more.
They both collapsed onto the sand, caught their breaths and had drinks.

"Wow" was all she could manage in between gasps of breath.
"You are a really great dancer" he smiled.
"You are not so bad yourself"
"I hope I didn't go to fast for you"
"No, not at all, I really enjoyed it"
"Good, I'm glad and I enjoyed it too"

They sat, enjoying the view for a while and resting in preparation for the climb back up the cliff side.

"Listen I'm doing a show at the beginning of next month, an end of summer showcase for my students to show what they have learnt and to raise funds to open my own dance studio and I was wondering if you would like to be in the show?"

"That's sounds great but I really don't think I'm ready for anything like that and besides I am heading home at the end of the month, back to reality you could say"

"I completely understand and hey the offers there if you change your mind"

"Thank you. I could have a go at helping you choreograph a routine if you like and maybe I can pop back down and watch your show from the audience"

"No problem and that would be great thank you"

"So you want to open your own studio"

"That's the plan"

"It sounds like a brilliant idea, I wish I could do something like that but I wouldn't have the confidence. So what's your plan then if you don't mind me asking?"

"No, not at all. Well I'm hoping to get enough money together to buy a studio and set up my own business"

"Wow that sounds great, I hope it works out for you"

"Thank you. Well we better be heading home"

A while later they stopped at the top of the cliff to catch their breaths.

"So Thursday, same place, same time and maybe we can work on that choreography too?"

"Sure and yes good idea"

"Great, see you Thursday then"

"See you Thursday"

CHAPTER TEN

After what seemed like ages, Thursday finally came round. Megan and Caerwyn met up again, had their picnic, went prawning then danced a rumba and made a start on the choreography for the show piece.

"That's looking good, we make a good team" he said as they sat on the sand for a rest.
"We do and I see what you mean about the rumba" she smiled slightly flushed at the thought of the rumba.
"Yes it really is a beautiful dance"
"I hope you don't mind but I have been thinking about your studio plans and I have an idea for you"
"No I don't mind at all and I'm intrigued now so you better enlighten me" he smiled with interest in his eyes.

"Well obviously it would cost more, but what if instead of just buying a studio you bought a whole building. I know that sounds like a lot but with a property that has studios, other rooms, a kitchen and a garden you could create almost like a community center. It could be a safe place for people to go when they want company or when they are struggling. A place for people with or without mental or physical problems to go and talk to people, even professionals or just do classes or read or just have company.

After all you and I both know how tough things can be and how important help and support can be. Anyway it's just an idea"

He sat watching her and mulled over her idea which she had just told him with so much excitement and passion. He suddenly realized she had finished and was awaiting his opinion.

"That's a brilliant idea"
"Really I was worried you might think it's too ambitious"
"It is but I reckon it is do able and people will go for it far more than just a studio. We should do it"
"Whoa, we, the idea was for you" she said shocked.
"Well yes but it is your idea so if you are interested we could do it together as a partnership?"
"It's a lovely idea but I'm going home at the end of the month and you've been brilliant getting me dancing again but a partnership in a business is a big step that I just don't think I'm ready for yet. I'm really sorry"

"I understand completely and there's no need to be sorry. I got a bit over excited that's all but just know that the offer is there if you change your mind at any point"

"Thank you and good luck with it" she smiled

They carried on with the choreography for a while longer then headed home.

CHAPTER ELEVEN

A few days later Megan and her granny had just finished eating their dinner.

"Are you ok Megan, only you have been a bit distant these last few days?" granny asked carefully.

"I'm fine granny, just mulling things over and trying to decide what I want in life. After all that's what this visit is for"

"Ah I see. Well I am a good listener and I'm happy to help in any way I can"

"Thank you granny I really appreciate that. It's just Caerwyn has offered me a partnership in his new business which I turned down but I can't help wondering if that was the right thing to do"

"I see, well only you can make that decision"

"I know it's just not easy. I mean I love it down here, I always have and it breaks my heart when I have to go home. That and I always said when I was old enough to live where I wanted I would move down here but it's a big step and I can't help wondering if it is the right thing to do"

"Well it seems to me that you are not entirely happy at home and you've been through so much there that maybe a change of scene and a fresh start is what you need but as I said it is your decision. Though if it helps you know you can stay here as long as you like"

"Thank you so much and you've given me food for thought there"

"You have got to follow your dreams and do what's best for you

"Do you know you are very wise granny?"

"Well I try my best"

They both sat deep in thought for a few minutes until Megan broke through their thoughts.

"You know what, you are right a change would do me good and it's my dream to live down here. Besides there is no harm in trying it for a while and seeing how it goes. If it doesn't work out I can always go back home"

"It sounds to me like you have made your decision and I will be glad of the company"

"Thanks granny you have been a great help and I really appreciate you letting me stay though if things do work out I will find my own place to live. Let's not tell anyone about this, especially Caerwyn, as there's a lot to sort out first and I think it would be better to get things in place before telling people"

"That's fine, I won't say a word and will leave it to you to tell people when you are good and ready"

"Thank you granny for everything"

"You are very welcome and if there is anything else I can do to help you just ask dear"

"Thank you and I will"

CHAPTER TWELVE

For the next few weeks Megan and Caerwyn met up, in their usual place, on his days off. They didn't have much luck with the prawns or the golf balls but their routine for the show was going from strength to strength and so was their friendship.

After weeks of prawning, dancing, talking and eating welsh cakes their last meeting before Megan returned home came. She still hadn't told him of her plans and had decided to tell him when she came back to watch his show.

They had agreed to meet in the same place as usual and as she walked towards him she could see that he was hiding something behind him on the wall overlooking the beach.
"Hello" she smiled.
"Hello, how are you?" he smiled back.
"I'm ok thanks. How are you?"
"Fine thanks"

"Go on then what are you hiding behind your back?"

"Oh dear you got me!! It's just a little something for you. Oh and before I forget here are two tickets for my show"

"Thank you and you really didn't need to get me anything. How much do I owe you for the tickets?"

"I wanted to and you don't owe me anything you are my special guest"

"Well if you are sure then thank you, I will do my best to be there"

"Great and this is for you but don't open it until you get home" he handed her the box he had been trying to hide with a purple bow on it.

"Thank you so much. I feel terrible now that I haven't got you anything"

"Please don't feel terrible it was just something I saw that I thought you would like and besides you have given me more than enough welsh cakes!!" he laughed.

"That's very true" she grinned

"Right let's make the most of our last afternoon together shall we?"

"Yes let's"

They ate their picnic then headed down to the beach. They started off with prawning and they found their luck had changed as they filled the bucket with enough prawns for a meal and they found a golf ball each.

"Well I think we can call it an overall draw as we both found two golf balls each"

"Deal"

They started practising their show routine. They moved across the sand with the sea lapping at their feet providing the music. As they came to the end of their routine they decided to add a few rumba steps to finish it. They moved carefully around each other, then Megan moved slowly away from him before he followed, turned her gently to face him and held her in his arms as if the dance was showing she was safe and cared for, the perfect end to the story.

She turned to face him, to tell him the new steps for the end were perfect, but stopped when her eyes met his. Slowly they moved closer, their hearts racing and eyes fixed longingly on each other. They were that close, they could feel each other's breath.

At that moment a piece of seaweed wrapped around Megan's ankle and she jumped back startled thinking it was a jellyfish.

Caerwyn grabbed her arm to steady her as a wave swept towards them so she didn't lose her balance. "Hey it's ok" he unwrapped the seaweed and held it up so that she could see it. "It's just a piece of rather slimy seaweed" he said as he threw it across the water out of the way.

"Sorry. I feel so silly, I thought it was a jellyfish"

"It could well have been, we were lucky it wasn't. You are not silly, you were scared and that's alright, I was scared too, though not just because of the seaweed monster!!" he winked.

She laughed. "What else were you scared of?"

"Well I was scared that I very nearly kissed you and risked our friendship, which I know sounds daft but your friendship means the world to me and you are going home tomorrow and I don't know when I will see you again apart from at the show. Oh dear now I sound like a right sob story" he said with a tear in his eye.

"Hey come here" she pulled him in for a hug. "You are not a sob story. You are a wonderful, caring man and your friendship means the world to me too. Besides we can write to each other and even visit each other. This is not the end, it is the beginning of a wonderful friendship" she smiled holding back the tears herself

"Thank you and you are right, a few hundred miles isn't going to get in the way of friendship" he smiled wiping his eyes.

"Now come on, you better get us back up that cliff before that tide causes a visit from the coastguard!!"

"Yes good idea"

They made their way back up the side of the cliff and then over to the wall where they had been meeting. Standing side by side they looked out at the view, the place that had seen their friendship grow.

"I will miss meeting you here" he said softly.

"Me too and you mean you will miss my granny's welsh cakes!!" she said with a giggle.

"Well of course, they are the best after all!!"

"They sure are" she agreed.

"But seriously I will miss you and our time together"

"I will too but we will see each other at the show and we can visit and keep in touch with each other"

"I better get some paper and pens sorted then!!"

"Yes you better and thank you so much for all your help and support, for listening, for getting me down and up the side of that cliff and for getting me dancing again. I really do appreciate it and you have really helped me find myself again as well as face a few fears!!"

"You are very welcome and thank you for listening to me, supporting me, giving me business ideas, teaching me prawning and for helping me find myself again too. Oh and for bringing me welsh cakes!!"

They hugged each other.

"True friends who keep in touch" he said.

"Yes true friends who definitely keep in touch"

They exchanged contact details and hugged one last time.

"Have a safe journey home and I will hopefully see you at my show"

"Thank you and I will try my very best to be there but I hope it goes well for you"

"Thank you and take care Megan"

"You too Caerwyn"

They started going their separate ways home but didn't get very far before they both turned, ran towards each other and hugged. After final goodbyes they tore themselves apart and headed home.

When Megan got home to her granny's, she emptied her bag and she came across the box with the purple bow on it that Caerwyn had given to her. She carried the box up to her bedroom and sat on her bed with it. She remembered he had said it was for opening when she got home. Carefully she took the bow off and lifted the lid off the box. Inside was something wrapped in purple tissue paper and a note on top of the tissue paper. She read the note.

Megan
I saw this and remembered your dreams and hoped it will make them come true.
I do so hope to see you at my show and perhaps you can debut this.
With all my thanks.
Take care and Best wishes
Caerwyn
xx

She carefully unwrapped the tissue paper and lifted out the most beautiful purple Latin dress.

She couldn't believe her eyes. It was better than anything she had ever dreamed of.

Her eyes filled with tears.

She carefully tried it on and it fit perfectly.

He really had made her dreams come true and she hoped she could do the same for him in return.

CHAPTER THIRTEEN

A week later and the evening of the show had arrived. Caerwyn and his team of helpers had been busily setting everything up and he was now waiting backstage for the audience to take their seats. He so hoped Megan would be in the audience as he really wanted to see her again.

Megan and her granny made their way into the hall to find their seats. Her granny had been only too happy to except the spare ticket to have a night out and Megan was glad of the company. She was looking forward to seeing Caerwyn again and was hoping to find the right moment to tell him of her plans including that she was staying.
Once everyone was seated the lights were turned down low and the room fell silent.
Megan could fell herself getting nervous for Caerwyn and hoped it would all go well for him.

An upbeat tune came through the speakers and the deep red silk curtains rose slowly revealing an array of dancers, in black outfits with bright coloured ties for the men and matching coloured flowers in hair and on skirts for the women.

They danced a free, energetic salsa with mambo's and rolling hips a plenty.

It was a great choice to kick off with and the entire audience danced, sang along and clapped in any way they could. Even her granny was up and dancing though Megan was a little worried about her over doing it.

Once the song finished the dancers bowed or curtseyed and then left the stage as the curtains dropped. After a few seconds the curtains rose to reveal a figure.

"Who's that?" Granny asked her.

She didn't answer but she knew it was Caerwyn hiding behind his disguise. She knew why he was doing it and she couldn't help wishing he could be himself.

"Well that was energetic, I wonder where that came from?" he said looking backstage then he turned to the audience. "Oh I am sorry I didn't see you all there, now where are my manners" he said with a searching look. "Ah yes. Good evening ladies, gentlemen, girls and boys"

The audience laughed and Megan enjoyed watching his cheeky side.

"Thank you all so much for joining us and we hope you are thoroughly entertained for the evening. Before the dancing takes over I would just like to take a few minutes just to explain why this show is taking centre stage.

My name is Anton, since a young age I have been passionate about Ballroom and Latin dancing, which has had its difficulties and I have had to face some challenges because of it. But that passion never leaves you and I came to realise that I wanted to help others to enjoy it too. So with that in mind I decided I wanted my own studio.

But then I made a special friend who gave me an idea. Instead of just a studio why not buy a whole building, to give people a place to go for support or just to find a purpose and give the community a helping hand in times of need.

So that's what I would like to do to help myself and the community but I don't want to do it alone, I want you the community to do it with me. So tonight isn't just about entertainment and donations, which are very gratefully received, it's about helping each other in our times of need"

The audience gave him a big ovation, clapping and cheering. Megan smiled knowing she had helped him find his way to his new adventure.

"Well that's enough from me for now, let's get on with the show. Now where have those dancers got too?" he said as he left the stage looking for them.

The audience laughed and clapped. The curtains went down behind him and then a calm soothing tune played out. Curtains up and on came the dancers and there he was, dancing with a beautiful lady. They lead the other dancers in a wonderfully graceful waltz. She also saw the couple she had followed to the hall that night she had tried to go to the classes. They had come on leaps and bounds with their dancing. Megan thought how elegant it was with graceful, slow turns, smooth gliding and the perfect choice of music to accompany it.

After the waltz was a paso doble with magnificent cape work and the story of the matador showing through with great power and the intensity of stamping feet and sharp turns.

Next was a trip to a Carnival through a samba. The dancers wore brightly coloured outfits with ruffles galore. Their hips shaking through whisks and samba walks. The music so catchy and fun that the audience couldn't help joining in the fun shaking and dancing in any way they could.

After all that fun they were in need of a rest so a slow Tango brought the first half of the show to a close. The sharp steps with flicks of the head and legs made for a powerful, intense tango.

There was a half hour interval after that, which Megan and her granny were pleased of. They both stood up.

"These seats could be a little more comfortable on the bottom!!"

"They sure could" Megan said while looking around for Caerwyn.

"I think I will go and get a hot drink. Would you like anything?"

"No I'm fine thank you granny. Can you manage?"

"Alright dear and yes I can manage thank you. You go and see if you can find Caerwyn if you like" she smiled.

"Yes I think I will. See you shortly" she said as her granny moved away.

At that moment a figure came bounding through the small crowd in the aisle. It was Caerwyn and he came up to her, smiled and gave her a big hug.

"I'm so pleased you came"

"So am I"

"Have I made a complete fool of myself yet?"

"No, not at all you were brilliant and your dancers were too"

"Thank you, that really means a lot coming from you"

He noticed the purple dress hidden underneath her bolero. "You like the dress then?" he asked casually.

"Yes sorry I meant to say thank you so much, it's perfect and it did make my dreams come true but you really didn't need to"

"I wanted to and you look stunning"

"Thank you, you scrub up well yourself" she smiled.

"Thank you"

At that moment the lady he had been dancing with joined them.

"Anton it's nearly time for curtain up"

"Yes, right I'm on my way"

The lady dancer flounced off.

"Sorry I should have introduced you, that was Cerys, my dance partner for the evening"

"I see and don't worry I know you are all busy"

"Caerwyn is that you?" granny exclaimed as she joined them.

"Yes, hello, it's lovely to see you and thank you for coming this evening"

"It's my pleasure and such a wonderful show you are putting on"

"Thank you and I'm glad you are enjoying it. Anyway I'm afraid I am going to have to go and get ready, but I will come and find you at the end of the show" he smiled.

"Good luck with the rest of the show" granny said looking puzzled at the wig he was wearing, but decided not to ask.

"Yes break a leg, though not literally of course!!" Megan chipped in.

They all laughed then Caerwyn headed backstage and Megan and her granny went back to their seats.

CHAPTER FOURTEEN

Caerwyn was waiting backstage. He was so happy that Megan was in the audience and boy did she look stunning this evening. That purple dress fit and suited her short, slim figure beautifully and her soft blonde hair in an up do complimented it perfectly. He had noticed she never wore make up but she didn't need to as her face was perfect without it.

The curtains suddenly went up and it was show time. The second half of the show opened with the cha cha.

Megan loved the cha cha, such an upbeat dance with simple chasse's, new yorkers and turns.

Next up was the rumba, which was beautifully danced and Megan could understand what Caerwyn meant about it being a captivating dance. It was a slow, sultry, tale of seduction.

"That dance gets you hot and bothered just watching it!!" granny said while wafting herself.
"You are not wrong there granny" Megan laughed. "The rumba is known as the dance of love" and it's Caerwyn's favourite she thought to herself.
"Oh well at least the male dancers are good looking!!" granny winked at her.
"Granny!!" Megan laughed.

A smooth, elegant foxtrot followed that took you to the musicals, with a mix of slow and quick steps and turns danced effortlessly.

Now it was the penultimate dance and it was Megan's favourite dance the jive. chasse's and kicks, fast and upbeat with the crowd on their feet. A small part of her wished she was up on the stage dancing with them but she knew she wasn't ready for that just yet.

The dance came to an end and the audience settled back down into their seats. The curtain came down while the stage was cleared.

Megan knew there was only one dance remaining, the one she and Caerwyn had choreographed together. She was looking forward to seeing it performed on the stage and hoped the audience enjoyed it as much as they had enjoyed choreographing it.

At that moment Caerwyn appeared on stage dressed in his usual sharp suit.

"Hello, me again. I promise to keep it short this time"

The audience smiled.

"Right where are we? Oh yes the last dance of the evening, thank goodness for that I'm ready for a sit down!!"

The audience laughed.

"Oh no I said that out loud" he said covering his face with his hands before removing them again.

"Let's try that again. "I hope you are all enjoying yourselves this evening?"

The audience cheered and clapped in an excellent response.

"Thank you, I'm so glad to hear that. We have now come to our last dance for this show and we hope it will be a fitting, enjoyable finale.

For this dance I wanted it to be something meaningful to the audience and to the show but at first I didn't know what that could be or where the show was going.

I then met a special friend, who showed me a path for the show and helped me follow it. She and I have helped each other learn to cope with difficult situations and through doing this we created this dance that you are about to see.

This dance is about helping people with mental and physical difficulties and those without, which is exactly what we aim to do with our centre, if we can get it up and running, which with all your help and support, we hope to achieve.

So this dance is for you" he smiled and went off stage while the curtains lifted.

The curtains lifted and Caerwyn came on stage, slowly walking up to Cerys who was wearing a coat over her dress as they had imagined. He held out his hand and she went to take it but drew her hand away again so he tried again to get her to dance with him and this time she did. It was perfect just as they had imagined it. She took her coat off and put it to one side before turning to face him.

Caerwyn looked at Cerys in the purple dress, then at the audience and then back at Cerys. This isn't right he thought to himself, it should be Megan up here and we should be dancing our routine together. He had already got everything ready in the hope that when he saw her in the interval he could convince her to dance their dance with him only he had decided against trying as he didn't want to lose his best friend or dent her new found confidence, but he realised now that she was the one he wanted to dance this dance with not Cerys. He knew this was his chance and he had to try.

With that he stopped and turned back to face the audience.
"I'm really sorry about this and I'm sorry to you too Cerys but there is something I need to make this dance perfect"
He went backstage leaving a stunned Cerys and the audience wondering what he was going to do next.

After a few minutes he appeared back on stage with a box and carefully walked down the stage steps and along the aisle through the middle of the audience towards where Megan was sitting.

Oh no please go back on stage Megan thought with panic setting in as he came towards her. Her stomach was in her throat and her heart was pounding as he reached her and stopped.

He smiled at her and mouthed "It will be ok"

She tried to smile back but she didn't feel very reassured.

Then he turned to the audience. "I'm sorry for the disruption but when I told you I had a special friend who helped me create this dance, I didn't tell you she is here tonight" he looked towards Megan.

"Ladies, gentlemen, girls and boys, this is my special friend Megan and this dance wouldn't have been created if it wasn't for Megan and neither would I have had the confidence to do this and to Megan and the audience's surprise he took off his wig.

She couldn't believe it, he was finally being himself and facing his fears.

"I want you all to know the truth.

My name is Caerwyn not Anton and I have been hiding behind this disguise because I was afraid of school bullies disapproving of my passion for Ballroom and Latin dancing, saying I must be gay because of it and it didn't stop at that, they also pushed me down a staircase which left me with a knee injury and fearing that I would never dance again.

Thankfully and with a lot of hard work I am here dancing today"

The audience clapped and gave him an ovation.

Knowing she would be too nervous to do it herself, he whispered to her

"Would you like me to tell them about your disability too?"

He caught her off guard but his courage made her want to try and be brave too.

"Ok" she whispered nervously and he smiled and squeezed her hand to let her know he was there for her.

"Thank you so much, that means a lot. Now before we continue, Megan has given me permission to share her story too.

Megan was a passionate Ballroom and Latin dancer in her childhood until at the age of just 16 she was diagnosed with arthritis from the waist down and like me she didn't think she would ever dance again.

Then after years of struggling, she met me and I helped her dance again. So you see we have both struggled physically and mentally but we never gave up our passion for Ballroom and Latin dancing and we have learnt that it is good to talk and be yourself. It was our stories that inspired us with the idea for the studio and for this dance"

He smiled at Megan, held his hand out to her and waited.

Slowly she put her hand in his but then she panicked and took her hand out of his.

He walked away a few steps and then stopped, turned and walked back towards her, handing her the box he had been carrying.

Megan looked at the box and carefully opened the lid. Slowly removing the tissue paper she gasped as she saw the contents. A pair of silver dance shoes just like the ones from her childhood. She couldn't believe it, first the dress and now the shoes.

She looked up as he started walking away towards the stage. He had done all this for her and now it was her turn to be brave.

"Caerwyn wait" she said nervously as she put the shoes on her feet.

He turned and smiled as he hurried back towards her and held out his hand again.

She put her hand in his and stood up. He carefully turned her round so he could help her remove her bolero.

As she turned back, a video of their spot started playing on a screen with sounds of the sea in the background. She was speechless, tears filled her eyes and without a word they slowly moved towards the stage hand in hand.

Once they were on the stage together, they floated effortlessly in a waltz. Turning and gliding then they changed pace to a cha cha and then went even faster with a jive.

All the time, telling their story of two people conquering their fears and sharing their passion for dance, in their own little world and both forgetting they were being watched.

After the jive they slowed things down to a rumba with beautiful slow movements and pure emotions. Then he gently lifted her in the air like lifting a trophy in celebration and carefully placed her back down so they were facing the audience. They moved around each other then she moved slowly away from him before he followed, turned her gently to face him and they looked lovingly into each other's eyes almost as if they were going to kiss. After a few seconds he took her in his arms and held her as if she was safe and they had faced their fears together, a perfect end to the story shown through dance.

The sound of the sea faded and the room was silent and tears of emotion flowed.

After a few moments the audience gave them a huge ovation, clapping, whistling and cheering, including Megan's very proud granny.

Both Megan and Caerwyn's hearts were thumping and their eyes filled with tears. They had done it and they had achieved more than they had ever dared hope for.

Neither moved for several moments and then Caerwyn gently whispered "Do you think you can manage a curtesy?"

"With you anything" she whispered back.

Together they faced the audience and Caerwyn took a bow while Megan curtseyed.

After a few moments the curtain came down in front of them with the audience still clapping and cheering.

"You did brilliantly" he smiled.

"Thank you and so did you" she smiled back.

"Thank you. Listen I need to do the closing speech so you head backstage and I will catch you up shortly"

"Ok" she looked around and he pointed her in the direction of backstage.

She headed backstage but stopped at the side of the stage, out of sight but close enough to hear his final speech of the evening.

The final curtain went up and Caerwyn was sweeping the stage. What on earth was he going to do now Megan wondered as she watched on.

"Can we get this place tidy as I'm sure we are all ready for home" Caerwyn said while sweeping the stage floor. He suddenly turned to the audience and put a hand over his mouth.

"Oh dear I am so sorry I forgot to finish the show, what am I like"

The audience and Megan laughed.

"Right" realising he was still holding the sweeping brush he tossed it to one side.

"Hey careful that nearly hit me!!" one of the male dancers shouted.

"Sorry" he shouted back and the audience laughed.

"Anyway where was I? Oh yes. Sadly we have come to the end of this show and this wonderful evening spent entertaining you all. On behalf of myself and everyone involved in tonight's show I would like to thank you all for coming and we all hope you enjoyed our show"

The audience clapped and cheered.

"I would also like to thank you for any support and donations you are able to give towards the community studio project.

As I said earlier this is a project that is close to my heart and I hope to get it up and running as soon as possible so we can try and help people and with your help we can do that.

This is our project and I want us to do it together so if anyone would like to get involved please let me know.

Anyway thank you again for a wonderful evening and hears to many more. Safe journey home everyone" he bowed and the audience applauded as the final curtain came down.

Megan headed backstage to wait for Caerwyn. As she wandered past the dressing rooms she stopped at the mention of her name and listened.

"Who is that Megan girl? She dances ok but if she has got arthritis I doubt she will be dancing much longer and what about Anton not being who he says he is!!" one of the dancers said.

"Hang on a minute, don't you see it doesn't matter who they are, what matters is that they both found the courage to stand up and share their disabilities with us and then show us that passions don't end where disabilities start they just adapt to new things"

Megan couldn't believe her ears, she didn't expect Cerys to stand up for them after Megan had taken her place in the final dance but she was grateful for her moving words all the same.

It didn't stop Megan thinking the other dancer was right about the arthritis, after all Megan didn't know how she would feel from one day to the next or how long she would be able to continue to dance or even walk for.

Tears stung at the back of her eyes at the thought and she knew she needed to re think her decision about moving to Wales.

She pulled herself together and wiped the tears away as she didn't want to spoil Caerwyn's evening. She would bid him good night and take her granny home as she must be tiring by now.

She headed out to the hall to look for her granny.

After a brief glance around the hall she spotted her granny talking to a couple of other ladies and headed over to them.

"Megan" Caerwyn called out too her as she got halfway across the hall and she stopped while he joined her.

"Hey, great closing speech. I'd love to chat but I have to get my granny home before she gets too tired"

"Thank you and thank you so much for dancing with me. I think we have been incredibly brave this evening" he replied smiling.

"We have but listen I've really got to get going" she smiled back.

"No problem, I understand but perhaps we can meet up before you go home?"

"Perhaps. Goodnight Caerwyn"

"Goodnight Megan"

She rushed off, collected her granny and headed home.

Caerwyn couldn't help noticing that Megan didn't seem quite herself but he thought she was probably just overwhelmed and trying to take things in, just as he was himself. He was back at work on Monday so he would leave it until then to give them both time to get their heads around things.

CHAPTER FIFTEEN

Monday morning came and Megan and her granny had just finished breakfast.

"Are you alright Megan? It's just you've been quiet and not yourself since we left Caerwyn's show on Saturday night" granny asked carefully.

"I guess I'm not really" Megan replied and then she explained what she had heard whilst backstage at the show.

"I can see why we left so hastily now and I can understand you not wanting to speak to Caerwyn until you have got your head straight. I know things aren't easy for you but that Cerys girl has got a point. You mustn't let your disabilities get in the way of your passions, you just need to find a way to adapt" granny said caringly.

"Thank you granny, I know I can count on you for good advice"

"You are very welcome and you know I'm always here for you if you need anything"

"Thank you that really means a lot but right now I think I'll go for a walk and clear my head"

"Ok would you like some company?"

"Thank you for the offer but if you don't mind I think I need a little time alone to gather my thoughts"

"I understand, you go and do what you need to and I will see you back here later"

"Ok see you later granny"

Megan left the house and headed off deep in thought.

She walked along the back road up towards the farm at the top of the hill. When she got to the top of the small hill she sat on the bench and looked out at the view across the fields, with the heritage coast in the distance.

As she sat there her thought turned to the situation she was in. she could move here to south wales and fulfil her dream to live here but then there was the matter of Caerwyn and the dance studio to think of or she could go home and make the best of it.

Moving here and having a fresh start was what Megan really needed after everything she had been through but she couldn't help thinking about what that girl had said that night backstage at Caerwyns show.

The girl was right, Megan didn't know how much longer she would be able to dance or walk and Caerwyn has been such a great friend to her but it's not fair to put him through that or to slow down his new studio venture, especially when he has got his own difficulties to cope with as well.

Neither of them knew what would happen with their disabilities and Megan knew that whatever she decided, she didn't want to lose Caerwyn's friendship.

Granny was just going to check if there was any post in the box when someone knocked on the door. She carried on to the door and opened it to find Caerwyn waiting.
"Hello Caerwyn, how are you today?"
"Hello and I'm not too bad thank you and you?"
"Oh well I'm not so bad myself"
"I'm glad to hear it. Is Megan in only she left rather quickly on Saturday night and I just wondered if she is alright?"
"I'm afraid you just missed her as she has gone for a walk to clear her head"
"Ah not to worry. I don't suppose you know why she left so quickly the other night do you?"
"Actually I do but it's not my place to say. All I can say is she heard something that really hit home and she is trying to sort her future out. But you will have to talk to her about it as it is really not my place. I'm really sorry"
"Please, there is nothing to be sorry for, I completely understand and I shouldn't have asked you"
"Thank you. I will say one thing though, Megan obviously thinks very highly of you and I really don't want to see her get hurt"
"I really appreciate that and I would never hurt her. She is a really special friend to me and I will be forever grateful for all the help and support she has given me. The truth is from the day I met her, here on this very doorstep, I have been falling in love with her but I'm scared to tell her as I don't want to lose an amazing friendship"

"Well I don't know what to say. I knew there was a spark between you both as I saw it when you danced together on Saturday night!!"

"You did!!"

"Everyone did, so it was either that or you are both very good actors!!"

"Thank you, I'm glad the story showed as it felt so very real to me. I just wish I knew how to tell her how I feel without ruining things"

"Well they say that the best way to tell someone how you feel is to show them and with your talent I'm sure you could find a way to do that"

"You're right and you've given me an idea but I will need your help" he exclaimed with joy.

"Well of course I am more than happy to help in any way I can"

Caerwyn told her his plan and what she could do to help and she agreed whole heartedly.

"So when is Megan due to go home?" he asked hoping he would have enough time to put everything in place.

"She is due to travel back on Sunday"

"Great, shall we say Saturday afternoon then?"

"That sounds perfect to me and hopefully we can get everything ready in time!!"

"Fingers crossed we will. So I will leave Megan a note asking her to meet me on Saturday afternoon and take it from there, that's if she turns up!!"

"That's fine and I will do my very best to persuade her"

"Thanks and thank you so much for helping me with this too"

"You are very welcome now hurry and get back to work before you get into bother for slacking!!"

"That's a good point. I will write her a note and leave it in the post box for her tomorrow"

"No problem, I will tell her you asked after her and leave it at that. Good luck with it all"

"That's great and thank you so much"

"My pleasure now go on get going"

"Yes I'm off, thank you and see you later"

"You are very welcome. See you later"

Megan wasn't sure how long she had been sitting on the bench trying to make a decision but she knew she was getting nowhere with it, so she gave up and walked back to her granny's house.

She walked in and shouted to let granny know she was home.

"Hello, did you have a nice walk?"

"I did thank you, though I'm still not sure what to do for the best"

"I'm glad you had a nice walk and I do hope you find the answers you are looking for soon."

"So do I granny"

"Oh before I forget, Caerwyn was here earlier with the post, he asked after you and he said he hopes he will get a chance to see you before you go home"

"That's nice" she replied before heading off to get sorted.

The next morning Megan brought the post in and found a note from Caerwyn.

She always loved finding notes in the post box from him but this time she wasn't sure if she even wanted to read it.

"Is that my newspaper" granny called as she came into the kitchen.

"Yes granny it's here" she passed it to her.

"Is there any post today?"

No just this note for me from Caerwyn" she murmured.

"Well aren't you going to read it?"

"I don't know. I just don't know what to do except try not to hurt him but whatever I do that could happen"

"I know it's not easy, but maybe you should read it and see what he has to say and who knows it might help you make your decision"

"I guess you are right as always" she smiled at her granny.

"I'm not always right but I do know a thing or two"

"You sure do"

Megan unfolded the note which read:

Megan

Sorry I missed you yesterday and I hope you had an enjoyable walk.

I am also sorry we didn't get a chance to talk properly after the show on Saturday night and I was worried when you left so quickly too. Though I expect you were extremely overwhelmed as I know I was too and with that in mind I thought I better give you some time and space to get your head around things, so that is why I haven't been in touch sooner.

Anyway I was hoping you might like to meet up one last time before you head home. I really don't want to put any pressure on you so I will wait at our usual meeting place on Saturday at the usual time of 1pm, if you come that would be lovely but if you choose not to I completely understand, wish you all the best for the future and I thank you from the bottom of my heart for everything you have done for me and for being the most wonderful dance partner I have ever had the pleasure of dancing with.

I also want you to know that you really are a true friend and I hope you will keep in touch.

Take care and hopefully see you soon.

With very best wishes.

Caerwyn

xx

P.S. Follow your dreams and remember you can always adapt them!!

With a tear in her eye she passed the note to her granny to read to.

"What a lovely note. That young man obviously thinks the world of you"

""You think so?"

"I do. I saw the way you two looked at each other when you danced together and there was more there than just friendship. You mark my words"

"Maybe"

"No maybe about it. So are you going to meet up with him?"

"I don't know, my heart wants to, but my head keeps saying maybe it is best to leave him alone so we can both move on"

"I know it is not easy but they say you should follow your heart and as Caerwyn says follow your dreams and adapt. From what I have seen and heard you and Caerwyn have got a very strong, special friendship which it is better to have that support than not to have anything so I really don't think you should give that up but it is your decision and I am here for you no matter what you decide"

"Thank you granny I really appreciate that and you are right there's no reason Caerwyn and I can't be friends and move on with our lives too. I think I might go and meet up with him after all"

"I think that is a very wise decision"

CHAPTER SIXTEEN

Saturday morning dawned and Megan found her granny reading her newspaper in the kitchen.

"Good morning Megan"

"Morning granny"

"How are you today? All ready for this afternoon?"

"I don't know, I still can't help wondering if meeting up with Caerwyn is such a good idea. I mean wouldn't it be better just to leave things as they are and just write him a note explaining things?" Megan said holding back the tears.

"I know this is difficult for you and yes you could do that but at the same time you could find yourself regretting not seeing him and telling him how you feel"

Oh granny why is falling in love never easy?" she asked and then suddenly realised what she had said clasping her hands to her blushing face in shock.

"There, you have finally admitted it though not to the right person I might add" granny said winking at her with a cheeky but caring smile.

"You knew?!" she exclaimed shocked at the thought.

"Well of course I did. I had my suspicions for a while and then I saw the way you gazed into each other's eyes and I knew my suspicions were right. I think you are wonderful together"

"Thank you granny. Now I have said it out loud it feels even more real"

"Then you should tell him how you feel"

"What and risk a really good friendship over a few silly feelings?"

"It's those silly feelings that often mean the most and a strong friendship makes for an even stronger relationship"

"I guess you're right"

Listen why don't I come with you this afternoon, I can get my friend to drive us down to the carpark and wait in their car with them while you go and meet Caerwyn and that way you have moral support on hand if you need it?"

"I'd like that thank you but only if it is not too much trouble"

"It's no trouble at all. I will phone my friend right away"

"Are you sure this, I mean meeting up with Caerwyn is the right thing to do granny?"

"Only you know the answer to that, but just don't end up with regrets"

"Alright the least I can do is say goodbye if nothing else, I owe him that much"
"Exactly and I will be with you all the way"
"Thank you granny"
"You are welcome"

Megan went upstairs to get ready while her granny made the phone call to arrange that lift for them both.

She sat on the bed and noticed the purple dress hanging in the wardrobe and the box of shoes underneath.

She got up and opened the box.

Caerwyn did all this for me, to make my dreams come true. She smiled.

Maybe granny is right and he feels the same way I do, she thought and then went back to getting ready.

At quarter to one their lift arrived and they made their way down to the carpark.

Once they had arrived her granny took Megan's hand in hers.

"You got this. Just be brave and follow your heart. I'm here if you need me"

Thank you so much granny and thank you for the lift" she said to Granny's friend in the driver's seat.

"You are very welcome" granny's friend replied and they both wished Megan the best of luck as she got out of the car.

Megan walked slowly up the path, past the remains of the castle, towards the meeting place.

As she got closer she could see Caerwyn waiting by the wall and stopped out of sight to gather herself together.

After a few moments she carried on walking towards him and stood by his side.

He turned towards her and their eyes met, stilling them both, neither saying a word until suddenly they both turned away and looked out to sea.

For a few moments neither of them knew what to say so just quietly admired the view along the heritage coastline.

After a while they both spoke "I'm sorry"
"Sorry ladies first" Caerwyn encouraged.
"Thank you. Well I was just going to say sorry for leaving the show so quickly. What were you going to say sorry for?" Megan asked puzzled.
"Well I was going to say I'm sorry for not getting in touch sooner. Also your Granny said you heard something at the show but don't worry she didn't go into any details"
"That's ok there is no need to apologise, you already told me why you hadn't been in touch in your note and I'm really grateful, as I did need time and space to deal with things in my head, so thank you.

As for the show, I really don't mind granny telling you and yes I did hear something.

One of the dancers was talking to the others about my arthritis and that I might not be able to dance for too much longer, but I don't blame them after all they were only telling the truth.

So please don't go upsetting them as actually they have done me a favour and helped me look at things in a different way and besides Cerys stood up for both of us which was really kind of her after I took her place"

"Oh Megan I'm so sorry, I wish you had told me but I respect your wishes and I won't say another word about it and as for Cerys that surprises me too but I guess we shouldn't judge a book by its cover and be grateful someone stood up for us!!"

"Thank you I really appreciate that"

"No problem. I will really miss this you know"

"What me rambling on?" she smiled.

"You're not rambling on at all, you are opening up and talking to a good listener and friend"

"If you say so"

"I do say so and I meant I will miss meeting up with you and talking"

"And these!!" she winked and pulled out a huge tin of granny's homemade welsh cakes.

"And most definitely those!!" he laughed and their gaze caught each other again.

"But seriously I really am going to miss you. This summer, meeting you and dancing with you has been truly wonderful and it's been the best summer ever. You have listened and helped me come to terms with my injury and pointed me in the right direction with the studio and my life.

So thank you so so much" he said holding back the tears.

"You are very welcome and I really am going to miss you too.

This summer has meant so much to me too. I came here lost and alone but then I found you. You put me back on track and showed me how to live again. You helped me laugh, enjoy myself and conquer my fears and for that I am forever truly thankful from the bottom of my heart" she said and they both had tears in their eyes.

He stood looking at her, opened his arms and they hugged each other close.

After a few moments they broke apart and wiped the tears from their eyes.

"Megan?"

"Yes Caerwyn?"

"I was thinking perhaps we could go prawning and then we could have one last dance before you go?"

"You know we don't have to go prawning every time you want to dance!!" she laughed. "Besides we haven't got the net and bucket with us"

He laughed. "Well that's ok then and that's a good point, we wouldn't catch much without those, though we didn't have much luck with them either!!"

They both laughed and he held out his hand, which she took and hand in hand they set off and climbed down the path, on the side of the cliff like they had done many times over the last few weeks.

CHAPTER SEVENTEEN

Once they got to the bottom, they made their way over the rocks, dodging the odd rock pool and out on to the sand and their dancefloor, neither uttering a word.

They took their positions and as the sea moved they moved, dancing the dance they had created on that very spot and danced that evening at the show some days ago.

As they danced Caerwyn noticed Megan had tears in her eyes.

"Are you ok Megan?"

"Yes I'm fine. I was just thinking how I wish my dad could see me now, down here after everything that has happened with my arthritis"

At that moment he stopped their dance. "Turn around"

She turned around and there standing on the rocks at the bottom of the cliff path, was her dad, smiling with tears in his eyes.

She couldn't believe it, he was here watching her and she stood there in shock with tears running down her face.

She wobbled slightly and Caerwyn, concerned she might lose her balance from the shock, caught hold of her arm to steady her.

Her dad came towards her and gave her a big hug.

"Seeing you down here dancing and smiling again is wonderful, a moment I never thought I would see you achieve Megan and thank you Caerwyn so very much for helping her and making her smile again.

Her mother and I are so very grateful for this, unfortunately she is up at the top of the cliff as her head for heights is not so good" he said as he pointed up the cliff side.

Megan and Caerwyn both looked up the cliff side, but not only could she see her mum but all her family and friends too and Caerwyn got a surprise of his own too as not only were her family and friends there but his were too!!

"How? Did you do this?" she said looking questioningly at Caerwyn.

"Well yes but I had a little bit of help"

"Granny!!" They both said and then laughed.

"Yes but it would seem she went one step further and got my family and friends here too!!" Caerwyn said while recovering from the shock.

"You know it strikes me you have got all your family and friends here, a father, and a stunning location which is the perfect recipe for a wedding!!" her dad said suggestively.

"Dad!!" Megan exclaimed slightly embarrassed.

"He's got a point"

Megan turned to look at Caerwyn only to find him down on one knee, perilously close to the water's edge, holding a small box containing the most beautiful ring with a purple stone on it.

Again she was in shock.

"Megan, you are the most special, true friend to me and from the moment I met you on the doorstep at your granny's house, I have been falling more and more in love with you.

I didn't know how to tell you, until your Granny gave me the inspiration and help I needed.

So in front of all our family and friends, in this amazing spot, our dancefloor and preferably before we get wet!! Will you marry me?" he asked with tears in his eyes.

"Yes" she cried with happiness and she gave him a hand to get up just before a wave broke at their feet.

"Perfect timing as always" he said carefully placing the ring on her finger, he replaced the box in his pocket for safe keeping and then took her in his arms and kissed her.

Suddenly remembering they were being watched, they moved apart.

"Are you ready?"

"As I will ever be, but what about the legal bit?" she said slightly worried.

"Don't worry about that, you can go to the register office to sort that out at a later date" her dad chipped in.

"Oh yes, I hadn't thought of that" Megan said relieved.

"Don't worry it doesn't matter that it is not legal and we are not wearing wedding outfits or anything else, all that matters is that we love each other and we are sharing that with our loved ones in a place that is very special to us" he said with tears in his eyes.

"He is right you know" her dad said in agreement.

"He is more than right, he is perfect" she smiled through the tears.

"Let's do this" they said in unison, wiped the tears away and looked up at their families.

Her dad took her across the sand and once composed and ready they walked arm in arm back across the sand to a waiting Caerwyn.

Knowing how nervous they both were, Caerwyn took the lead, only to her surprise he didn't speak just lead her first in a jive then in a rumba and that moment they and their loved ones knew words weren't needed as the dance said it all and there wasn't a dry eye on the beach including the sea!!

EPILOGUE

Megan did stay in South Wales after all and not long after their perfect wedding on the beach, Megan and Caerwyn got married officially, in the register office with their parents as witnesses.

After that they spent several months fundraising for their community studio.

They found the perfect building and with the help of many volunteers from the community and beyond, including builders, plumbers, electricians and other professionals they brought the community studio to life.

This project was something they worked hard on as it meant so much to them and their community.

Opening day had finally come and they opened the doors of their community studio and the hope of helping people.

After all the excitement of the day, Megan and Caerwyn found a quiet spot alone on her granny's doorstep, where they first met.

"We've done it" Caerwyn said joyfully smiling at their achievements.

"We sure have" she smiled back.

"I really hope that"

"The Coastal Expressions Community Studio"

"Yes, the Coastal Expressions Community Studio. I really do hope it helps people to talk and to not be afraid to reach out for support"

"I really hope so too, after all it was talking that brought us together and enabled us to help and support each other when we needed it most"

"That is so very true" he agreed, smiling at her.

"I also hope that through helping our generation to talk and reach out, we can help further generations in the future too and maybe one day our own children as well"

"I hope so too. By the way, did you oil your creaky hinges!!" he smiled cheekily.

She laughed "Perhaps we should try lifting the lid and find out!!"

Together they lifted the lid on the post box and there was the creak that started their friendship. They laughed.

"I didn't have the heart to oil them!!" she said.

"No it would be a shame to lose the creak" he agreed taking her in his arms.

They both spoke at the same time "The perfect conversation starter"

Printed in Great Britain
by Amazon